Who's Gonna Fill Their Shoes

Lindsay Jeter

To order additional copies of this book, contact:
Xlibris
844-714-8691
www.Xlibris.com
Orders@Xlibris.com

ISBN: Softcover   978-1-6698-7416-4
             EBook   978-1-6698-7415-7

Print information available on the last page

Rev. date: 04/12/2024

Summary

Have you ever wondered who your little ones are looking up to? Who they are, what they stand for, and so many other things? In today's world, our children are being influenced by many "idols" or "heroes" that are not necessarily the best role models for them. There are some really great influential people that are famous that are great role models for our children, but there are many that are not. Just because a person is not famous through the public eye, does not mean he or she can't be a good role model for our children. This children's book encourages children to look at heroes, or role models to look up to, all around them in everyday life. Firefighters that save lives from burning buildings, emergency room nurses that save lives from tragic accidents, next-door neighbors that deliver food when a young mother has just birthed her first born child, little girls setting up a lemonade stand on the street to sell Girl Scout cookies that go to a good cause, and so many more people that are in our everyday lives that go above and beyond their normal job or duties for the day to lend out a helping hand to make a difference in our lives are everyday heroes. So, this book encourages not only children to look up to the proper role models, but for parents to train up a child in the way, he or she should go, as the Bible teaches us to do. And, ultimately the hero that we should want to model after, and be more like every single day is the one who gave his life for us, Jesus.

Many heroes walk among us.

Some we pass in the store, and some give us the last seat on the city bus.

Some come from our church
and bring food to our door.

Some are small and set up their
own Girl Scout cookie store.

Some are big and put out the fires we can't.

While others show up to our games for support and give the loudest chants.

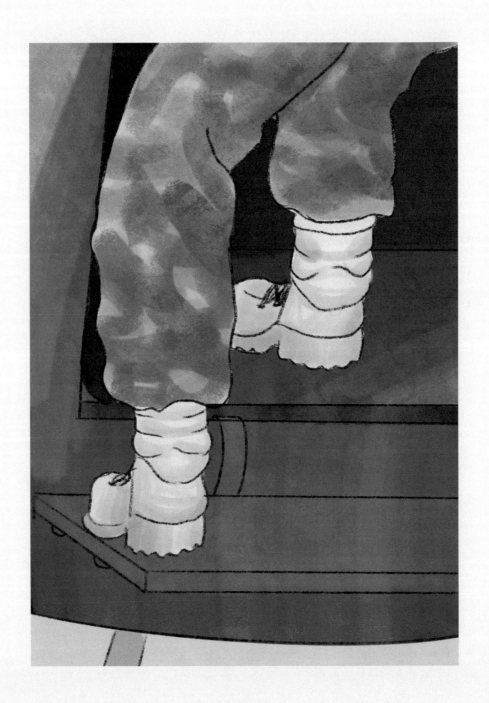

Some leave their families so we can be free.

Some work in hospitals to save
the lives of you and me.

There are heroes everywhere- one
may even live next door.

But, the most special hero that
ever lived gave us even more.

He died for our sins and rose again so
we can be in Heaven one day, too!

Have you seen any today? There
is also one inside of you.

Printed in the United States
by Baker & Taylor Publisher Services